lay forever on video and DVD

© Disney

Published by Ladybird Books Ltd.
A Penguin Company
Penguin Books Ltd., 80 Strand, London WC2R 0RL
Penguin Books Australia Ltd., Camberwell, Victoria, Australia
Penguin Books (NZ) Ltd., Private Bag 102902, NSMC, Auckland,
New Zealand
Copyright © 2003 Disney Enterprises, Inc.
All rights reserved.
LADYBIRD and the device of a ladybird
are trademarks of Ladybird Books, Ltd.
10 9
Printed in Italy

WALT DISNEY'S

CLASSIC

ALADDIN

Ladybird

Once upon a time, in the ancient city of Agrabah, there lived a ragged but handsome boy called Aladdin.

He was very poor and often became so hungry that he had to steal food from the stalls in the marketplace. But Aladdin was determined he would not remain a thief for ever.

He dreamed of better things. "One day, Abu," he promised his pet monkey, "things will be different. We'll live in a palace and wear fine clothes, not rags."

Meanwhile, in the Sultan's luxurious palace, time was running out for beautiful Princess Jasmine. Her father, the Sultan, was becoming very anxious.

"But dearest," he insisted, "the law says you must marry a prince before your next birthday. There are only three days left for you to choose a husband."

"The law is wrong!" cried Jasmine. "I don't want to marry anyone I do not love – even if he is a prince."

Jasmine fled tearfully into the gardens and hugged her pet tiger. "Oh Rajah," she sighed, "I don't want to be a princess anymore." Then she planned her escape.

Early the next morning the Princess disguised herself in a long cloak and climbed over the palace walls.

Jasmine made her way through the bustling marketplace. Seeing a hungry child, she picked up an apple from a stall and offered it to him. The Princess did not know that she ought to pay the fruitseller.

"Stop, thief!" shouted the man, rushing forward to seize the Princess.

But Aladdin, who happened to be passing, leapt to Jasmine's rescue. He led her to the rooftop where he and Abu lived. As he gazed at the beautiful young girl, he knew he was falling in love.

Suddenly the royal guards stormed up the staircase and arrested Aladdin.

"Release him, by order of the Princess!" Jasmine cried, pulling back her cloak.

"The Princess?" gasped Aladdin.

"I would, Your Highness," said the chief guard, "but my orders come from Jafar." And the guards dragged Aladdin away to the palace dungeons.

Now, Jafar was the Sultan's most trusted adviser. But, unknown to the Sultan, he was plotting to take over the throne. Jafar knew of a magic lamp that would give him all the power he needed, but it was hidden in a mysterious cave in the desert.

The Tiger-God that guarded the cave had told Jafar that only a *Diamond in the Rough* could enter the cave – someone whose worth was hidden deep within.

Using his magical powers, Jafar found out that this was Aladdin. So, disguised as an old beggar, Jafar freed the boy from the dungeon and led him through the desert.

Promising great wealth, Jafar persuaded Aladdin to enter the cave and get the lamp for him. The fearsome Tiger-God warned them to touch nothing but the lamp.

Inside the first chamber, Aladdin and Abu met a friendly magic carpet who showed them where to find the lamp. But just as Aladdin picked it up, Abu caught sight of a magnificent jewel in the hands of a giant monkey statue.

Forgetting the Tiger-God's warning, Abu quickly snatched up the jewel. At that very moment, the cave walls began to collapse and the floor gave way. Aladdin, Abu and the magic carpet were trapped.

When the earthquake had stopped, Aladdin studied the lamp. "What's so special about this dusty old thing?" he wondered, rubbing it clean with his hand.

Suddenly the lamp started to glow.

A cloud of smoke billowed from its spout and became an enormous shape with laughing eyes and a curly beard.

"I am your Genie, direct from the lamp," said the amazing creature. To prove it, he released Aladdin from the cave and offered him three wishes.

Aladdin thought of Princess Jasmine. She would never marry a poor street boy. "Genie," he said, "I wish I were a prince."

The Genie waved his hand and turned Aladdin into a prince, dressed in the finest silks. Abu became a magnificent elephant to carry Aladdin to Agrabah.

Calling himself Prince Ali Ababwa, Aladdin marched towards the Sultan's palace in a grand procession.

That night, Aladdin took Princess Jasmine for a moonlit ride on the magic carpet. By the time they had returned, Jasmine knew that at last she had found a prince she wanted to marry.

But Jafar had other plans. He ordered his guards to capture Prince Ali and throw him off a high cliff.

As Aladdin sank beneath the waves, the lamp fell from his turban. Using Aladdin's second wish, the Genie saved his master from drowning.

Back at the palace, the wicked Jafar
had hypnotized the Sultan using his
magical snake staff.

"You will marry
Jafar," the Sultan
ordered Jasmine in a
strange voice.

"Never! Father,
what's wrong with you?"
asked Jasmine.

"I know!" said
Aladdin, bursting
into the room.

He snatched the staff from Jafar
and smashed it to pieces. At once
the Sultan snapped out of his trance.

Jafar fled. But as he left,
he glimpsed the magic lamp
hidden in Aladdin's turban.

"So," thought Jafar, hiding safely in the tower, "Prince Ali is really that ragged urchin, Aladdin – and he has the lamp. But not for long!"

The next morning Jafar's cunning parrot, Iago, flew silently into Aladdin's room and stole the lamp.

"At last! I am your master now!" cried Jafar, as he rubbed the lamp and watched the Genie appear.

Reluctantly, the Genie obeyed Jafar's orders and made him the Sultan. Jafar then wished to be the most powerful sorcerer in the world.

Jafar cast a spell over the whole palace. He suspended Jasmine's father from the ceiling like a puppet and imprisoned the Princess in an enormous hourglass. He turned Aladdin into a street boy again and surrounded him with sharp swords.

Aladdin bravely took up one of the swords and challenged Jafar to a fight. In reply, the evil sorcerer conjured up a flaming wall of fire and turned himself into a huge cobra.

Jafar raised his head to strike Aladdin. "Did you think you could beat the most powerful being on earth?" he snarled.

Aladdin thought quickly of a way to trap Jafar. "The Genie has much more power than you!" he taunted.

The power-mad sorcerer knew that the boy was right. "Genie," he said, "my final wish is to be the most powerful genie of all."

A swirling mist of light surrounded Jafar, and he changed shape. Then Jafar and Iago were sucked into a lamp, which had appeared from nowhere. Like all genies, Jafar was now trapped for ever, a prisoner in the lamp. His evil spell was broken.

The Princess ran into Aladdin's arms.

"Jasmine, I'm sorry I lied to you," said Aladdin. "I'm not a prince at all – I'm only the poor street boy you once met in the market."

"But I still love you," sobbed the Princess. "I want to marry you! Oh, if it wasn't for that stupid law!"

The Genie appeared at Aladdin's side. "You still have your third wish left," he said. "I can make you a prince again."

Aladdin shook his head. "Genie, with my third wish, I give you your freedom. But I'm going to miss you."

"Me, too!" the Genie replied with a smile. "You'll always be a prince to me."

"That's right," the Sultan agreed. "You've proved your worth as far as I'm concerned. What we need is a new law. I decree that from this day, the Princess may marry whomever she wishes!"

"I choose Aladdin!" Jasmine cried in delight.

Aladdin took Jasmine in his arms.
They looked into the sky and watched
the Genie fly off to a new life of freedom.
They knew that they would all live
happily ever after.

Yours
to own
on ᗪᴉꜱᴺᴇᎽ
DVD

WALT DISNEY
CLASSICS

Magical stories t